Dear Parent:

Congratulations! Your child is taking the first steps on an exciting journey. The destination? Independent reading!

STEP INTO READING® will help your child get there. The program offers five steps to reading success. Each step includes fun stories and colorful art. There are also Step into Reading Sticker Books, Step into Reading Math Readers, Step into Reading Write-In Readers, Step into Reading Phonics Readers, and Step into Reading Phonics First Steps! Boxed Sets—a complete literacy program with something for every child.

Learning to Read, Step by Step!

Ready to Read **Preschool–Kindergarten**
• big type and easy words • rhyme and rhythm • picture clues
For children who know the alphabet and are eager to begin reading.

Reading with Help **Preschool–Grade 1**
• basic vocabulary • short sentences • simple stories
For children who recognize familiar words and sound out new words with help.

Reading on Your Own **Grades 1–3**
• engaging characters • easy-to-follow plots • popular topics
For children who are ready to read on their own.

Reading Paragraphs **Grades 2–3**
• challenging vocabulary • short paragraphs • exciting stories
For newly independent readers who read simple sentences with confidence.

Ready for Chapters **Grades 2–4**
• chapters • longer paragraphs • full-color art
For children who want to take the plunge into chapter books but still like colorful pictures.

STEP INTO READING® is designed to give every child a successful reading experience. The grade levels are only guides. Children can progress through the steps at their own speed, developing confidence in their reading, no matter what their grade.

Remember, a lifetime love of reading starts with a single step!

Visit us on the Web!
www.stepintoreading.com

Educators and librarians, for a variety of teaching tools, visit us at
www.randomhouse.com/teachers

Library of Congress Cataloging-in-Publication Data
Eliopulos, Nick.
Flying high / by Nick Eliopulos ; illustrated by Loston Wallace
    p. cm. — (Step into reading. A step 1 book.)
ISBN 978-0-375-85208-4 (trade pbk.) — ISBN 978-0-375-95208-1 (lib. bdg.)
I. Wallace, Loston. II. Title.
PZ7.E417Fly 2008 [E]—dc22 2007033040

Printed in the United States of America 38 37 36   First Edition

DC SUPER FRIENDS

FLYING HIGH

WITHDRAWN

by Nick Eliopulos

Illustrated by Loston Wallace and David Tanguay

Random House 🏠 New York

Batman swings
over Gotham City.
The sun is shining.

But something strange is in the air. The Super Friends have work to do.

Honk! Honk!

Pigeons block traffic.

Flash races
to the rescue!

The pigeons
fly away.

Caw! Caw!

At the beach,
seagulls steal food.

12

13

Aquaman
and his friend

make a big splash!

Squawk!

Ostriches run away from the zoo.

Superman and
Green Lantern
fly to the rescue!

They stop the birds
in their tracks.

Hmmm.

Batman spots a clue.

It is a strange machine.

Batman takes
a closer look.
The noisy machine
bothers the birds.

23

Now the birds
are happy again.

Inside, the Penguin

robs the bank.

"The Super Friends
are too busy!
They can't stop me,"
he says.

But Batman leaps
into action.

He stops

the Penguin's evil plan.

Teamwork
saves the day!

31